SAVIOUR PIROTTA
was born in Malta, where he began his career
writing children's plays for radio. He moved to the United Kingdom in 1981,
and is now a popular storyteller visiting schools
around the country. His previous books for Frances Lincoln
are *Little Bird* and *Joy to the World*.

NILESH MISTRY
was born in Bombay, India. He moved to Britain in 1975
and studied at Harrow School of Art and Central St Martin's School of Art.
His latest book for Frances Lincoln is *Nico's Octopus*,
written by Caroline Pitcher.

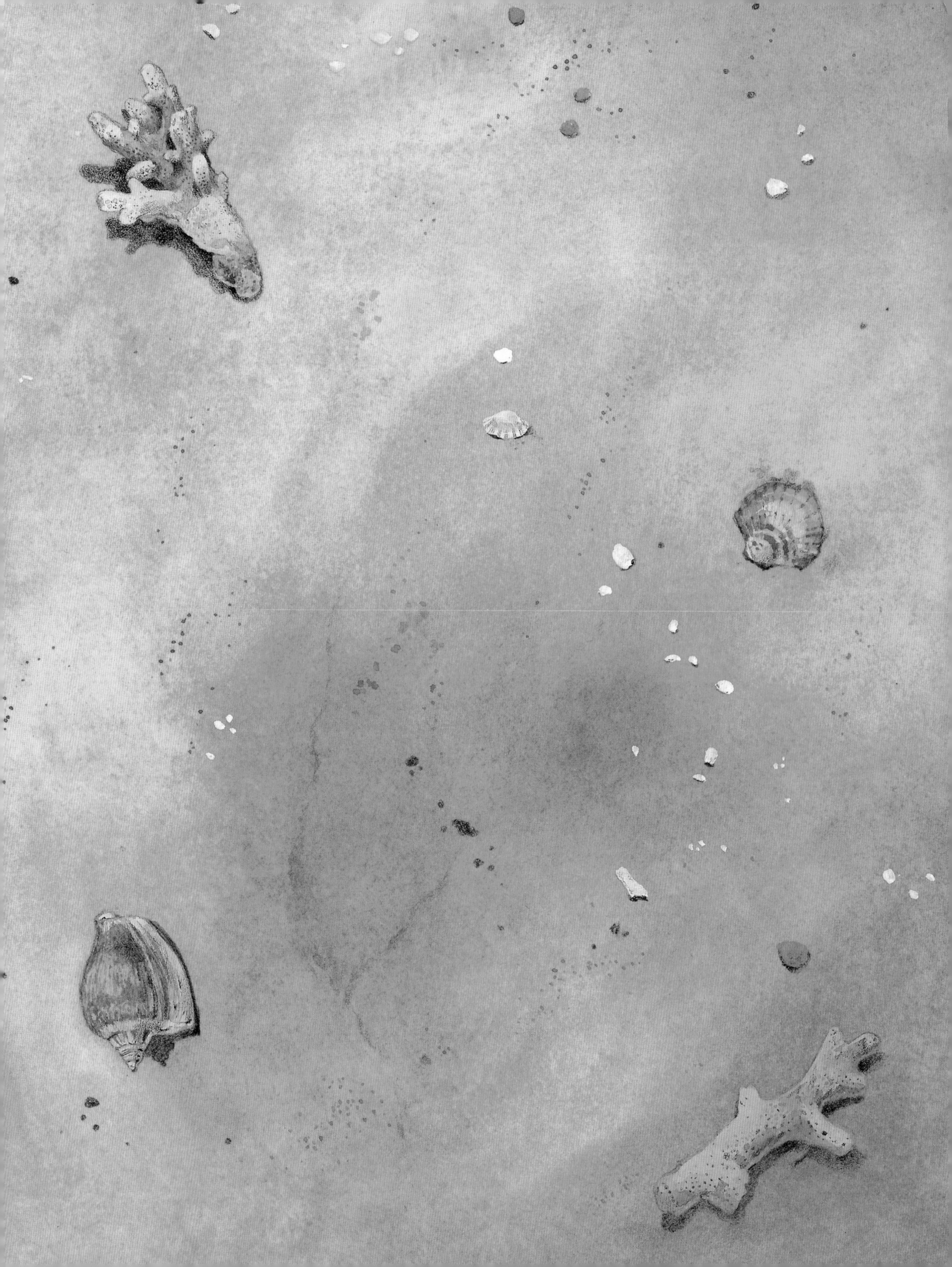

**For Fiona and Aimée – S.P.**
**For Balkrishna and Rasik Mistry – N.M.**

STORY BASED ON AN ORIGINAL IDEA BY YUKKI YAURA



First published in Great Britain in 1997 by Frances Lincoln Children's Books,
4 Torriano Mews, Torriano Avenue, London NW5 2RZ

www.franceslincoln.com

First paperback edition published in 1998
Distributed in the USA by Publishers Group West



British Library Cataloguing in Publication Data available on request

ISBN 0-7112-1168-X (UK)
ISBN 1-84507-411-4 (USA)

Printed in China
1 3 5 7 9 8 6 4 2

# Turtle Bay

SAVIOUR PIROTTA
*Illustrated by* NILESH MISTRY

FRANCES LINCOLN CHILDREN'S BOOKS

TARO and Jiro-San were friends.

Jiro-San showed Taro how to feed crabs with pieces of rotten fish. He taught him to dive for beautiful sponges. When the sea was too rough for swimming, he trained him to sit very still and watch the sea-horses swim around the seaweed in the deeper rock pools.

Taro's sister, Yuko, didn't like Jiro-San very much.
"He's weird," she said. "Last year my friends
saw him sweeping the beach with a broom."
"No, he's not," said Taro. "He's old and wise,
and full of wonderful secrets."

One day, Taro found Jiro-San sitting on a big rock.

"What are you doing?" he asked.

"I am listening," said Jiro-San. "The wind is bringing me a message." Taro sat on the rock and listened. But all he could hear was the seagulls crying.

"Ah," said Jiro-San at last. "Now I understand... My old friends are coming."

"Who are your old friends?" asked Taro.

"You'll see," said Jiro-San.

Next day, Jiro-San brought two brooms and handed one to Taro.

"For sweeping the beach," he said.

Taro's heart sank. Yuko was right after all - Jiro-San was weird.

"There's a lot of rubbish and broken glass on the beach," Jiro-San explained. "My friends won't come if there is broken glass. They know they'll get hurt."

The two friends swept the beach from one end to the other. They collected all the rubbish and put it in Jiro-San's old cart. Soon the beach was cleaner than it had been all summer.

Jiro-San looked pleased.

"Meet me by the big rock tonight," he told Taro.

Taro ate his supper as fast as he could.

"You seem in a big hurry," said his mother.

"I am," said Taro. "Jiro-San's old friends are coming."

"Who are they?" his mother wanted to know.

"It's a secret," said Taro.

"What kind of secret?" Yuko asked.

Taro didn't answer. He washed his hands and went out to find Jiro-San.

"Look," said the old man, pointing out to sea. Taro saw a school of dolphins riding the waves.

"Are they your old friends?" he asked.

"No," said Jiro-San. "Perhaps they will come tomorrow night."

Taro waited patiently all the next day. In the evening he met Jiro-San again. This time, the old man had brought his old boat out of the shed. Jiro-San picked up the oars and they pushed out to sea.

After a while, the old man said, "We've got company." Taro watched in amazement as a huge whale flicked her tail up out of the water. She had a young one swimming beside her.

"Are they your old friends?" Taro asked.

"They're friends," said Jiro-San, "but not the old friends I meant. Maybe they will come tomorrow."

The next evening, Jiro-San was in his boat again.

"Where are we going?" Taro wanted to know.

"Over there," said Jiro-San. He rowed out to a secret cove on a little island. There Taro saw three large fishes with swords for snouts.

"Are they your old friends?" Taro asked.

"All fish are my friends," said Jiro-San. "But these aren't my old friends. They seem to be late this year. Perhaps they are not coming at all."

"Don't be sad," Taro said. "Perhaps they'll get here tomorrow."

"Do you want to come and wait for Jiro-San's old friends?" Taro asked Yuko after supper the next day. Yuko wasn't doing anything, so she followed Taro to the big rock, kicking the sand as she walked.

"Ssshh," said Jiro-San. "I think they're here at last."
Yuko and Taro saw a dark shape moving towards the shore. It was huge and bobbed up and down on the water like an enormous cork.

At last the children could see what it was - a turtle!

"She's coming to lay her eggs on our beach," said Jiro-San proudly.

The turtle scrambled ashore and started digging with her flippers. When the hole was deep enough, she laid almost a hundred round, creamy-coloured eggs in the nest. Then she filled in the hole with her hind flippers, flung more sand over it with her front flippers, and hurried back to the sea.

"She is going to tell the others," said Jiro-San.

"What is she going to tell them?" asked Yuko.

"That the beach is safe," said Taro happily.

The next evening, Yuko came to the beach with a new broom.

"Can I help sweep the sand?" she asked.

"Of course," said Jiro-San. "The more of us there are, the safer the beach will be for the turtles."

The three friends swept up all the litter dropped by the holiday-makers during the day. Then they sat on the rocks and watched more turtles coming ashore. There were lots of them, all huge and old and wise - just like Jiro-San.

"Now," said Jiro-San, "you must be patient, and wait until you hear from me again."

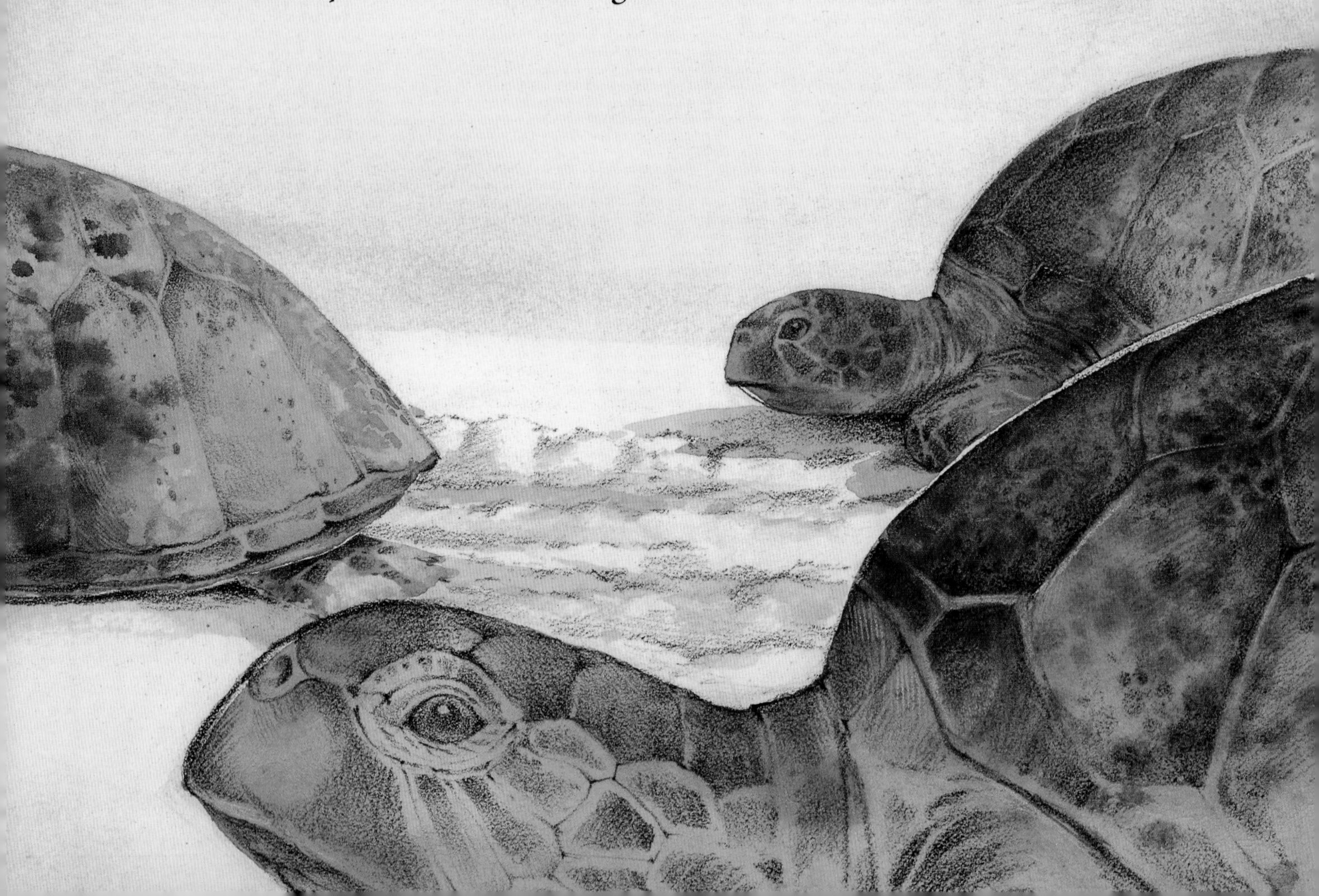

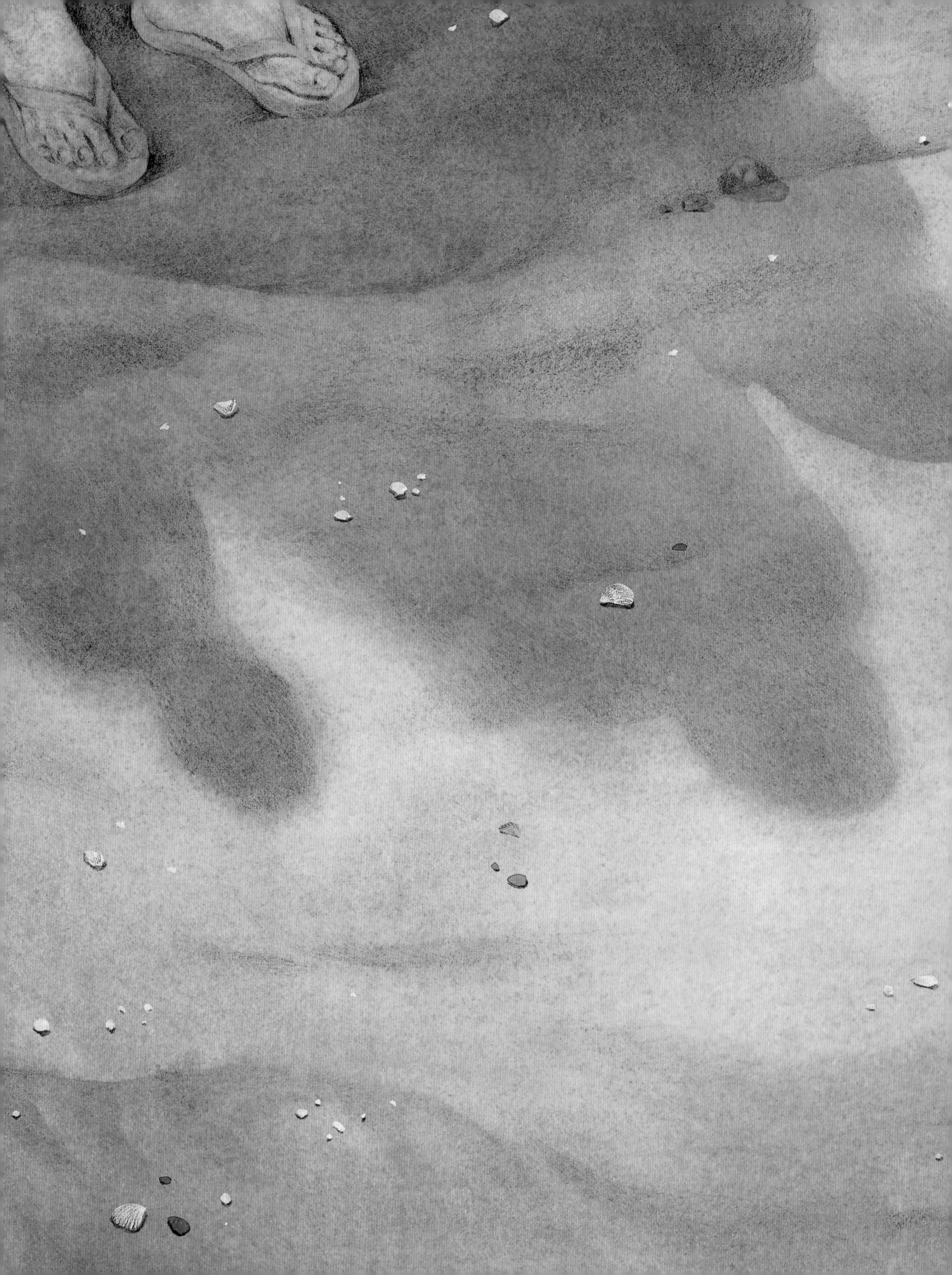

Eight weeks later, Jiro-San told the children to meet him at dusk.

"Sit on the rocks, please," he said, "and watch the ground."

The children looked and waited for what seemed like hours. As the moon rose, they saw something moving under the sand - something small and fast and eager.

"It's a baby turtle!" cried Taro. "The eggs have hatched!"

Soon the beach was full of baby turtles. There were hundreds of them, all scuttling down to the sea.

The children couldn't believe their eyes.

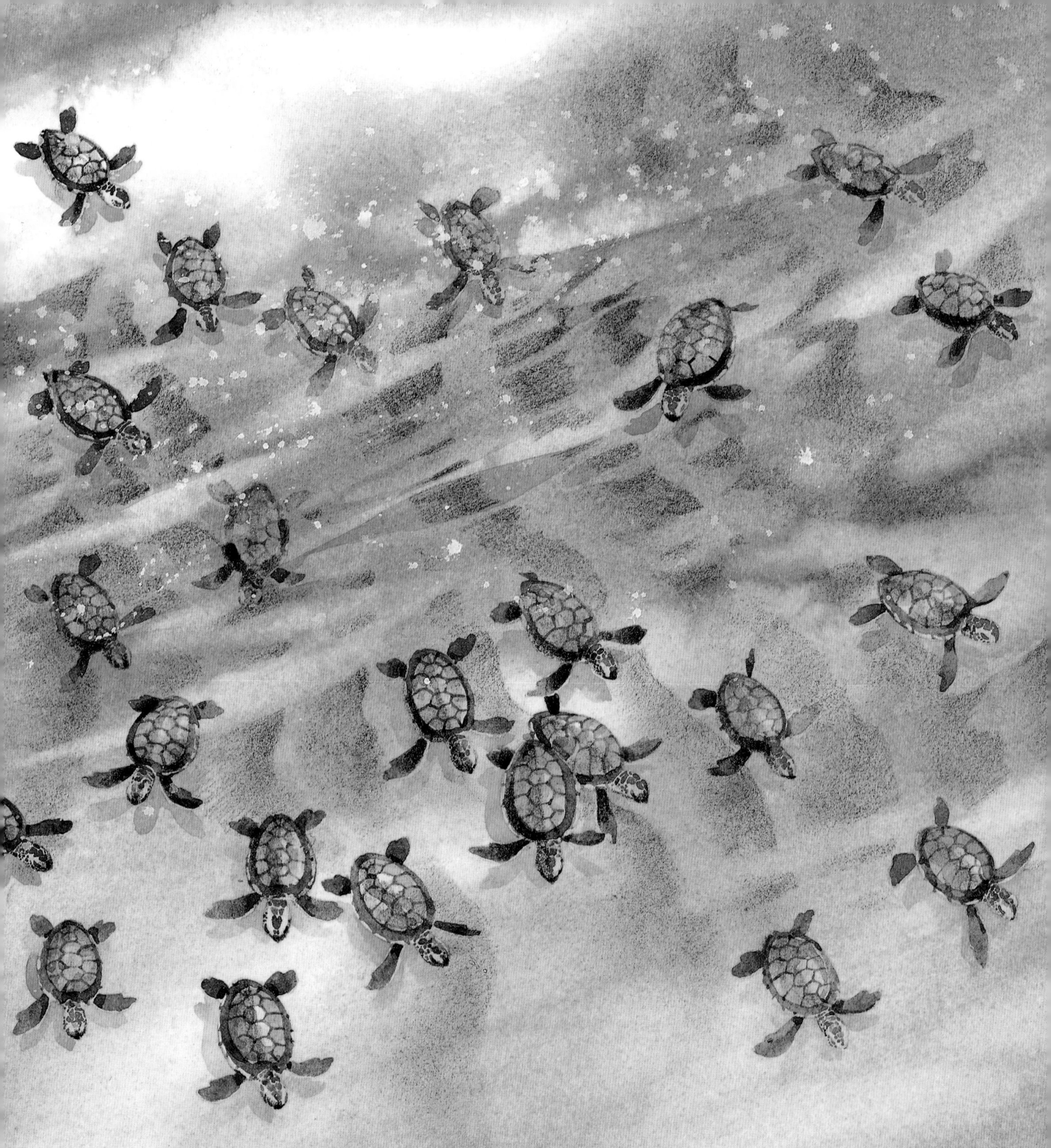

"Jiro-San is not crazy after all, is he?" Taro whispered to Yuko.

"No," said Yuko. "He is old and wise ... and full of wonderful secrets!"

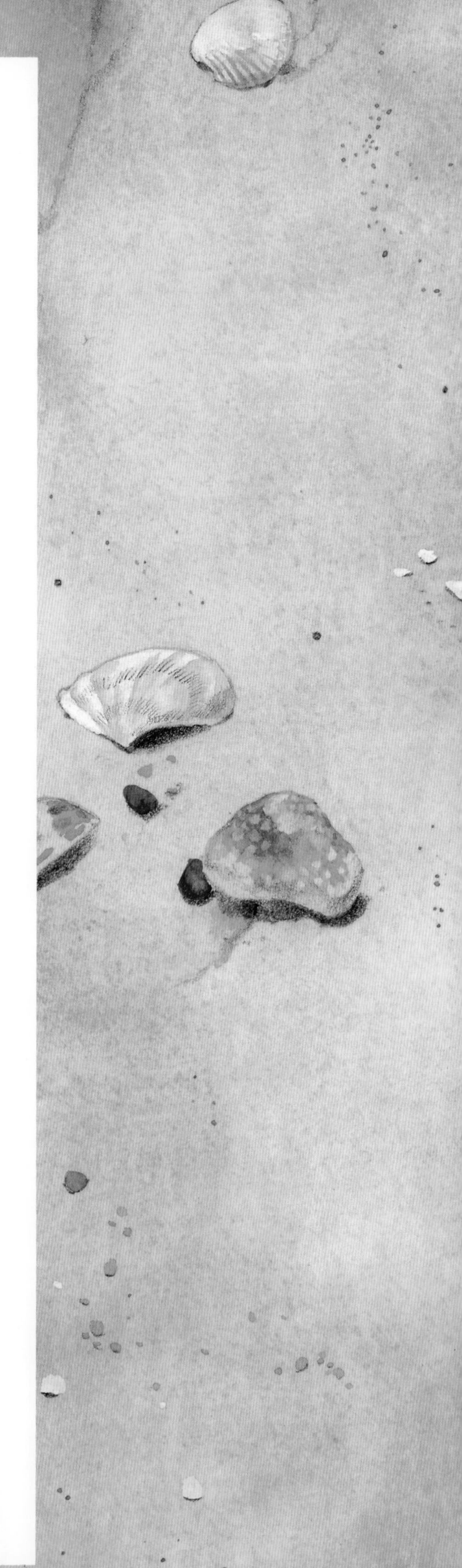

# About Sea Turtles

Jiro-San's old friends are loggerhead turtles, one of seven different kinds of turtles living in the sea. Although turtles are born on dry land and breathe air, they spend most of their lives swimming in the warm oceans, feeding on sea grasses, crabs, shrimps and shells. Like tortoises and terrapins, they have bodies that are protected by armour made of bones and horny shell.

When the weather is warm, loggerhead turtles migrate to shallow water to mate, and the females come ashore at night to lay their eggs on sandy beaches, using the same places that have been used for centuries.

Each female digs a bucket-sized pit with her flippers. Her eggs - 100 or more - have leathery shells so they will not break as they plop into the nest. She covers the nest with sand to hide it from greedy creatures such as lizards.

The mother turtle cannot survive long on land, so she goes back to the sea and takes no further care of her family.

After two months, the eggs hatch and the baby turtles push their way up to the surface of the sand and scurry down to the water. They usually go by night, for by day sea-birds and other enemies might catch them. Once in the sea, they can live for over fifty years.

Except for large sharks, adult sea turtles do not have many enemies, but some human beings like to eat turtle meat and to make things out of their shells, and turtles sometimes get caught in fishing nets. People also like to build hotels and spend holidays on the beaches where turtles lay their eggs, so in those places turtles have become very rare.

Conservationists are now trying to help protect turtles and their breeding-grounds.

MORE BOOKS IN PAPERBACK FROM FRANCES LINCOLN

## Yi-Min and the Elephants
## *A Tale of Ancient China*

*Caroline Heaton*
*Illustrated by Tim Vyner*

Yi-Min, smallest and most indulged daughter of the Chinese Emperor, longs to see an elephant. Her father agrees to take her on an elephant hunt and her wish is granted. But then the hunters raise their bows and arrows and Yi-Min's distress leads to a special birthday promise to protect the elephants for evermore.

ISBN 0-7112-1853-6

## Spirit of the Forest
## *Tree Tales from around the World*

*Helen East and Eric Maddern*
*Illustrated by Alan Marks*

Trees are symbols of life itself. We cut them down at our peril. Here is a leafy anthology of 12 traditional tales from all over the Earth's surface, from Native North America to New Guinea. The stories include tales of high magic, bravery and guile, death and rebirth, each woven around a tree.

ISBN 0-7112-1863-3

## The Vanishing Rainforest

*Richard Platt*
*Illustrated by Rupert Van Wyk*

Why is the Brazilian rainforest vanishing so fast? And why is it essential not only to the people and animals within it, but to the whole world? This story, seen through the eyes of a child called Remaema, describes how the Yanomami tribe are stIll battling against potential developers. Can a solution be found?

ISBN 0-7112-2127-0